More Tales of the Unusual

'true' mysteries past and present

Diane Madden

The Brucedale Press

More Tales of the Unusual

copyright 2002 Diane Madden

map copyright 2002 Norman R. Anderson

All rights reserved. No part of this work may be reproduced or stored by any mechanical, photographic, or electronic means without the written permission of the copyright holder, except brief passages quoted (with proper credit) in reviews or as references. Photocopying without permission of any of the material herein is an infringement of copyright.

Where characters and settings in these stories are based on living people and actual places, they are presented with the permission of the people involved, or from information in the public record.

The Brucedale Press was established in 1994 to publish quality books of local interest and literary, historical, or pictorial merit. Look for its publications at your bookseller's or order from

The Brucedale Press
Box 2259, Port Elgin, Ontario N0H 2C0

edited for publication by Anne Judd
cover design by Janice Coleman-Sanagan
printed and bound by Skyway Printing

National Library of Canada Cataloguing in Publication

Madden, Diane, 1959-

More tales of the unusual : "true" mysteries past and present / Diane Madden.

ISBN 1-896922-23-6

1. Curiosities and wonders—Ontario—Bruce (County). 2. Curiosities and wonders—Ontario—Grey (County). 3. Tales—Ontario—Bruce (County). 4. Tales—Ontario—Grey (County). I. Title.

GR113.5.B78M33 2002   001.94'0971318   C2002-903272-5

Created and produced entirely in Canada.

Foreword

Shaking my flashlight to prolong its weakening light, I lay with blankets tented over my head, tucked in around me lest some light leak out and be noticed by my parents who had not yet gone to bed. I was always ready with a finger to click off the light if I heard a tell-tale squeak on the stairs at the end of the hallway leading to my parents' bedroom.

This was how I enjoyed most of the ghost stories I read as a child, everything our school and local libraries had to offer. Nothing truly gory or gruesome, just chillingly spooky.

As an adult, I still like these books. Always on the lookout for something new, I decided to make my contribution to library shelves by researching and writing down local ghost stories, legends and folklore for others who share my taste for slightly spooky 'true' tales of the unusual. This is my second book. My first, *Tales of the Unusual,* has done exceptionally well. People send copies all over the world to family members who have moved from the area.

The stories are all told in fun and you may have even heard some of them when you were a child, or read them in local history books. Whatever your approach, I hope you will feel that same chill when reading them. I have had fun researching the mystery in our history and talking with people who were willing to share their stories with me.

More Tales of the Unusual

    This second book is again dedicated to my husband Bill and our children Bryan and Jennifer Madden, who put up with my hogging the computer room at times.

    I also want to thank the staff of the various public libraries I visited, as well as the staff at Bruce County Museum & Archives in Southampton, and the Grey County-Owen Sound Museum for their help. Thank you also to the people whom I interviewed and to those who gave their stories for others to enjoy.

    And, as my manuscript became this book, my thanks for the skills of map-maker Norm Anderson, cover designer Jan Sanagan, and editor Anne Judd.

Diane Madden   May, 2002

Contents

Fish Story? (Southampton) 7
Forewarning (Kincardine) 10
Georgie—Forever a Child (Mar) 12
Ghost in the Family (Saugeen Township) 16
Ghost of Seven Maples (Chatsworth) 18
Ghost Ship (Big Bay) 24
High-Water Mark (Stokes Bay) 28
Jerry—Just a Lifeless Dummy? (Southampton) 33
Justice Carried Out (Walkerton) 39
Light the Way (Craigleith) 42
Lingering Lavender (Mount Forest) 46
Phantom Piper (Kincardine) 51
Poltergeist (Paisley) 53
Prediction Fulfilled (Owen Sound) 56
Rest in Peace (Owen Sound) 59
School Section #10 (Glenelg Township) 64
Tarred and Feathered (Colpoy's Bay) 69
The Crying Boy (Oliphant) 73
The Curse (Elsinore) 76
Unidentified Flying Object (Clavering) 79
Underwater Wonders (Colpoy's Bay & Tobermory) 81
Where's Mom? (St. Edmunds Township) 85
Witching (Grey & Bruce) 90
With Help from Ma Bell (Sauble Beach) 93
Suggested Reading 96
About the Author 98

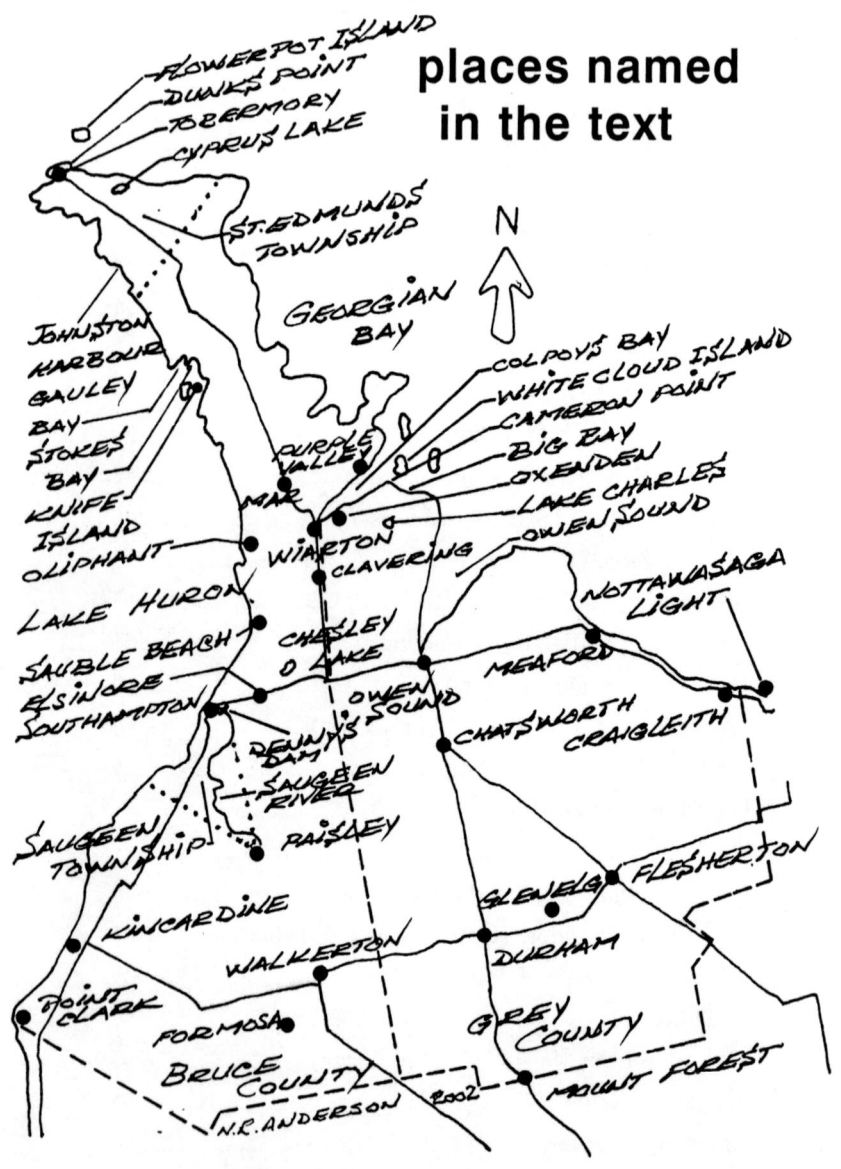

Fish Story

On the Saugeen River near Denny's dam the local fishermen nearly caught something that was far too big for their nets. Is this one of those fish stories that gets larger with telling, or is there a bit of truth to it?

In the late spring of 1989, a group of local fishermen were trying their luck on both sides of the Saugeen River. Above Denny's dam people enjoyed watching the fish try to jump and swim upriver to their spawning grounds. A woman, the wife of the witness, sat and dangled her legs over the edge, relaxing and enjoying herself.

The person recounting this story to me said that he was a witness to the spectacular events that quickly unfolded. Watching the fish jump the dam around noon that day, he spotted a large dirty brown object come over the dam in the rushing waters heading to Lake Huron. Expecting a large log, the man watched the water. What appeared was totally unexpected and unexplainable.

Instead of a log, a large brownish serpent-type animal reared out of the water toward the dangling legs of the unsuspecting woman. It seemed to rise about four feet out of the water, its reddish eyes glaring. What looked to be teeth showed in its open mouth and it appeared to have a head along the style of a bat's with little protruding ears. The beast had small arm-like appendages. Trying to judge the length, the man said it was about 30 feet. Because it was in the water, he had trouble making out the total length. He described its swimming style as undulating up and down, not slithering side to side as a snake does.

Fishermen on both sides of the river were also witnesses to this activity. They yelled at the woman to get out of the way while they were running away from the water, adding to the confusion. The husband of the woman had been paralyzed in a car accident and cannot walk. He called to her to get her attention, and threw objects out of the car where he was sitting to try to get the attention of the animal while his wife scrambled to safety. In total, although it seemed forever, the animal stayed up out of the water for less than 10 seconds, he guesses. The beast swam toward Lake Huron, with the people watching until bushes blocked the way. His wife jumped into their car and the couple tried to follow the river but the bush was too dense.

Alert for local talk or newspaper writeups during the next few days, the couple heard nothing of any significance. They have kept this to themselves for all these years, wondering if they actually saw what they thought they saw. It may have been a large tree trunk with branches stuck here and there, though the couple believe to this day that it was a freshwater monster of some sort. The man can still sketch a picture of this serpent as it is so fresh in his mind.

Who can tell what unknown species may lurk beneath the waves? After all there have been many strange sightings over the years in various cold-water rivers and lakes. In the past, fish could be

More Tales of the Unusual

caught in great quantities, though now their numbers are diminished by overfishing, pollution and the changing of the waterways.

Massive sturgeon were caught in and near the Saugeen and photos show them standing as tall as a man. Perhaps this is what came over the dam that day—a monster from the past.

Forewarning

Only a few decades ago many a small town lad grew up with the thought that someday, when he matured, he'd venture off to sea. As Kincardine, Ontario, is on the shores of Lake Huron, this was a common idea amongst male children of that area during the late 1860s. John Quinn was no different. His story was published in the Yearbook of the Bruce County Historical Society, a great place to glance back at excerpts from the past.

John, the son of an Irish immigrant family, had set his sights on joining the crew of one of the lake boats that regularly sailed from Sault Ste. Marie to Detroit, calling in at the bustling port of Kincardine. Most immigrant families brought over their old customs and beliefs with them to the new world. These traditions kept alive the memories of their ancestors and of the land of their birth. The Quinns were a musical family as most were. At least one or two members of a household in years past could play a musical instrument. John was quite skilful, possessing his own violin. Family legend says that the life of an ancestor was saved by a violin which played music by itself, a forewarning that told in advance of something about to happen. Belief in the supernatural was commonplace amongst the immigrants. This too came with them from the Old Country.

More Tales of the Unusual

Early one morning in 1868, at the age of nineteen, John decided that today was the day. He got up, washed, dressed, ate, and was off. He had not informed his mother of his intentions, but as he walked into Kincardine, the young man knew his future lay before him. Though he had little experience, John convinced the captain of a boat to hire him. He would start the following day.

John's father was already at the harbour. He had walked in earlier that morning, having some business in town. John met up with his father and told him of his plans to leave the next morning, as he had been hired on as crew on a laker. As they discussed the future, they both noticed Mrs. Quinn striding toward them. She was dressed all in black. She stopped in front of the two men. Facing John, she said, "I know you've been hired by the captain of this boat to work for him. You are *not* to go. After you left this morning, your violin played a tune, and you are not to go on that boat."

John was astounded at what his mother had just said. So convincing was she, and knowing family tradition, John had no problem deciding to stay home the next day. Why tempt the fates?

The next morning, the ship John had signed on with left without him, sailing onto Lake Huron. Word came back later that as the boat neared Goderich, a fierce storm had come up. The vessel was wrecked and all aboard drowned.

Thanks to a message from beyond, John Quinn lived on to enjoy his future as a crew member of another laker, sailing safely between Sault Ste. Marie and Detroit for several summers after that.

Georgie—Forever a Child

When a death is sudden and traumatic, there is a belief that what may have been the essence of that human life hangs around, not realizing they have passed on to the next realm. Some of these "ghosts" may be seen, heard, smelled, felt or all of the above. It seems to depend on the receptive psychic ability of the person who comes in contact with the ghost. Such may be the case in a home in the Mar area, in Bruce County.

In a large farmhouse, built around the turn of the 20th century, a household member who lived there in the early 1980s recalled to me, very vividly, her ghost story. As a mother of young children, she was aware of where they were playing, ready to run to them at any sign of problems. She soon came to realize that there was another child in the home as well, though not of this world. Although she had never seen the child, she just sensed, in her mind's eye, that it was a young boy, four or five years old, with curly blond hair and blue eyes. The name Georgie seemed to fit the young ghost. It is thought also to be the name of a child who lived in the home many years ago.

The family would hear a ball bouncing on the wooden floor, and when someone went to look, nothing was to be seen. The ball could be heard to

More Tales of the Unusual

bounce along the floor, hit one particular door and bounce back, the laughter of a young boy accompanying it. Sometimes, laughter would ring throughout the whole house. It was a happy sound, not frightening. The laughter could be a nuisance as it was sometimes heard above the television, even when the volume was turned up louder and louder by those listening to it.

Once in a while, stranger things would happen. A skipping rope went missing when its owner put it down for just a moment. When potato chips were served as a snack, one bowl would be emptied when mother's back was turned, before it had been given to the children. It got so that the mother filled three bowls of chips, to save her children accusing each other of eating their chips. When guests came over, the ghost was part of the entertainment. A bowl would be filled with potato chips, the mother would leave the kitchen and then go right back into it. There would be no sign of the chips!

Some days the sound of a child's footsteps would be heard running up and down the stairs. The two-year-old child in the family heard the footsteps one day. He questioned his daddy as to who was playing on the stairs. Daddy said that it was Mommy and that she had better stop it. Just then, Mommy called from another bedroom on the same floor, wanting to know what she should stop. Daddy didn't have anything else to say.

The last time Mommy heard the child was around 1984. When she came home from buying groceries in town, she saw that her husband was quite pale and very quiet. She asked him what was wrong.

More Tales of the Unusual

Taking her aside, he stated that although he didn't believe in ghosts and wouldn't admit to believing in ghosts, there was definitely *something* in the house. He told her that as he was watching television, the laughter became unbearably loud. He had turned the volume of the TV as loud as it could go to try to battle the sound, to no avail. He had blown up in anger and yelled that this was his house and to stop laughing and smarten up. The sudden silence had deafened him.

The child was heard no longer. As she moved from the home shortly after that occurrence, the woman is not sure whether the present owners still hear the ghostly child.

Farms are usually passed down generation to generation and, as in many small towns, people knew the former owners of the home. After making contact and talking with one of the former family members of the home, the woman learned that a boy about four years old had been killed some time in the early 1900s in the farmyard. Curiosity had gotten the better of him, and though warned about the dangers of the barnyard, the child had ventured too close and had been butted by a ram and died. He was buried in the front yard under the big old tree, where his heartbroken mother could gaze upon his grave and watch over him, comforted by the fact that he was still with her, if only in spirit.

That same woman who told me the story recalled a depression in the front yard, under a large tree. The ground always seemed to be sunk down. She tried to fill it in with earth various times, but the spot would always sink down again. Possibly this was the boy's grave, but as records were sparse in the early 1900s, no one knows the exact spot, and out of respect, the earth was never dug up to find out.

She also recalled one day long ago when she lived there, hearing the sound of a young child, crying. The sound continued for about twelve hours. No cause for the strange sound could be found. Possibly it was the anniversary of the ghost child's death or a forewarning of things to come. No one knows.

Perhaps the child is still playing in that happy place where he lived out his short life, unaware of how much time has gone on without him.

Ghost in the Family

A 'friendly houseguest' is the description given to an unseen member of a Saugeen Township family. The following story appeared in a local paper, The Beacon Times, *January 1996.*

A farmhouse owned by a local family has been the location of many unexplained events. Although quite sure the 'entity' is a friendly male ghost, they are never aware of what is going to happen next.

Although they have lived in the home for less than ten years, it is only in the last three or four years that the family has noticed increased sightings and strange incidents.

The father of the family was the first to see the apparition, which looks like a well-dressed male, in a relatively modern style of clothing, with a long-sleeved shirt and pants. The "ghost" vanishes as quickly as he appears.

One day, hearing footsteps upstairs, and knowing that no one else was home, Mother bravely entered the living room to investigate. She stopped dead in her tracks as her gaze caught sight of someone at the top of the staircase. He disappeared! She knew right away this was the ghost and instantly became a believer in the supernatural.

The apparition has been seen, similarly dressed, by various other members of the household. The ghost appears to be a young man, in his early thirties, with dark hair and about five feet, seven inches tall. He seems to favour the living room, as he has been seen near the fireplace, perched on the edge of the arm of the couch, looking very life-like. The ghost appeared very content, staring into the glow of the warm crackling fire.

The teenage daughter of the family blinked upon seeing him, not quite believing her own eyes. He was still there when she reopened them. He then instantly disappeared. Though not afraid, she realized that he was a ghost.

The family have accepted their unseen member. Hearing strange footsteps, doors opening and closing, and ghostly sightings have become almost commonplace. As they cannot solve the mystery of the being in their farmhouse, they live together in harmony, enjoying their house guest. Someday they may find an answer.

Ghost of Seven Maples

An author friend told me the following story.

It was December 23, 1985, and a cold wind whispered around the corners of the Evans family home just two kilometres south of the village of Chatsworth, Ontario. Originally built in the 1800s and added to over the years, the house had seen many a pre-Christmas night—but not many like this one.

Normally a good sleeper, the fourteen-year-old daughter of the family was having a nightmare. This was not a common occurrence for her. In the dream, she was deep in a dry, stone-lined well, unable to escape. She could see a circle of dim light high above her head, but just couldn't get a toe-hold on the stones of the wall. Looking down again, she could make out the skittering shadows of what appeared to be rats, running around her feet and climbing up the walls toward her face. Panic-stricken, she slapped out at the moving shapes, knocking down some of the hairy beasts but more kept crawling up in front of her eyes.

A loud crash made her jump, startling her out of the nasty dream. She sat bolt upright in bed, her eyes staring, her body shaking from the effects of the nightmare and the sudden awakening. The old swag lamp just outside her open bedroom door was lit, but almost immediately she heard the pull-chain rasp through the small opening in the socket and the lamp went out. Fumbling for the small flashlight on her bedside table, she turned it on and crept out the door into the now-darkened living room. The swag lamp swung slightly as if a hand had just left it and the chain tapped the bulb gently with every swing but she knew there was no one else downstairs.

Mum and Dad slept upstairs, and the old wooden steps creaked very audibly whenever someone went up or down. Wendy was alone on the ground floor but not for long. Within a few seconds she heard her mum stirring and saw the stairway light come on. Mum came down the creaky stairs, tying her robe tightly against the cool air.

Her mother asked Wendy about the loud crash, as it had awakened her as well. Wendy had no idea what had happened so together they peered around the door of the kitchen where the sound appeared to have come from. They were unable to see much by the dim glow from the upstairs light. They tiptoed through the kitchen to the back door, turned on the switch and flooded the whole room with fluorescent light. Wendy glanced at the clock on the stove and saw that it was 5:30 a.m.

A startled gasp made Wendy look at her mother, who was pointing nervously across the room.

Though the two women had just crossed the kitchen, they had not stepped on anything. A large wooden plaque, carved with a rooster weathervane motif, was lying on the floor in two pieces. It had been hung on the wall the previous spring, with small nails and strips of double-sided tape. The body of

More Tales of the Unusual

the bird had gone across the kitchen, striking one of the almost-new pine chairs, making a sizeable dent in the edge of the seat, and now lay almost beneath the chair. The tail of the rooster had slid along the floor in another direction and was resting by the dishwasher, about ten feet from the chair. There was no sign of the little nails that had held the plaque, but traces of the double-sided tape still clung to the plaque and to the wall. Strangely, the two adhesive sides of the double-sided tape appeared to have been forcibly pulled apart.

Not having any real explanation for finding the bird on the floor and not really being scared by the strange event, they soon stopped thinking or talking about it, but there have been several unusual things heard and seen since that time.

One particular morning in the spring of 1989, Mum had just come in from working all night at the nursing home, and Dad was leaving soon for his job. They were eating breakfast together at 7:30 and Wendy was still asleep in her room.

"Listen to that child's breathing!" the father exclaimed. Wendy was suffering from a cold at the time and when great, slow, gasping breaths sounded throughout the kitchen, he thought of her immediately. After all, who else could it be? Concerned for her daughter, Mum went into the living room and stood quietly by Wendy's bedroom door. Wendy's breathing was noisy, yes, but both her quicker breathing and the louder, slow, rasping sounds could be heard as distinctly separate sounds.

First the loud breathing seemed to be coming from the cellar-way, of which one wall adjoined

Wendy's bedroom. After listening, both parents agreed that the sounds were not being made by Wendy. But when they went to stand in the cellarway to listen, the noise seemed to be once again coming from the girl's room itself.

Wherever the baffled pair went in the old house, the harsh breathing sounds seemed to come from somewhere else. After five or six minutes the breathing started to become fainter and finally stopped altogether. When Wendy awoke later on, she had no recollection of the curiously loud, raspy breathing, nor any strange dreams which might have helped explain things.

There was no explanation to come: possibilities, such as it being a windy day outside or the old house groaning and creaking, or even the air whistling down a chimney, were all quickly dispersed. No, nothing so easily understood.

Another episode of the loud breathing sounds occurred in the fall of 1990, when Wendy and her maternal grandmother were inside the house alone. Wendy was alone indeed, at least in one way, for Gram was completely unable to hear the breathing, and scolded her granddaughter for trying to scare her when Wendy, truly frightened, mentioned the breathing. Again, the location of the sound was impossible to pinpoint and the noise faded away after just a few minutes.

Years seemed to go by between manifestations of the ghost at Seven Maples, if it was in fact a ghost. Maybe things did occur, but they were not impressive enough to remember. The last time a memorably strange thing happened was in the summer of 1996. A few of Wendy's friends were visiting, and they were moving throughout the living room, the kitchen, and Wendy's old room, which was now Dad's office and computer room. Wendy's father and one of her friends were in the computer room, while Wendy, her mother and another friend were watching TV in the living room. Suddenly a man's shadow seemed to saunter through from the kitchen swinging its arms just as one of the young guests might. As a shadow is a common thing, no one thought anything much of it... until later.

For some reason something started to bother the three people as this happened again, several times during the evening. Becoming curious as to who (or what) it was, as there is usually a person attached to their shadow, they checked around the house, but each time all visitors were accounted for. Weird? Yes, but there was no unusual explanation or any real cause for worry.

A few days later, Wendy's father saw a man's shadow standing just inside the garage door, but when he turned around to greet his visitor, there was no one there, nor was anyone in the yard. The dog lay quietly in his usual place; if someone had in fact come to visit, the dog would have announced them as usual.

Of course there has been much discussion among family members about these strange occurrences, but no explanation can be found for them. Wendy seems to be a common factor in almost all of the manifestations. Youthful energy does seem to have a "draw" for different types of supernatural happenings, sometimes known as

More Tales of the Unusual

poltergeist activity. Such noisy, mischievous energy is sometimes said to be caused by the hormonal energy surrounding adolescents.

Trying to come up with explanations for their strange experiences was not easily done, though there may be some connection to the original house. The basement of the old house extends only under the kitchen and dining room, which, along with the bedroom / computer room, were part of the original log home. Though they have never checked, to this day the family wonders what might be under the linoleum tiles and the plank floor of Wendy's old room.

Perhaps having active teenagers in the home attracted some type of poltergeist activity, or did Wendy's nightmare have a connection to the unexplainable happenings—a message she was meant to understand; perhaps a grave from before the old cabin was built; perhaps an old, dry well, responsible for someone's untimely death remains under the floor. It just may be that a shadow from the past lingers on, not quite aware that life has gone on without him. Or he may be coming back from time to time to check on things. No one knows for sure, but as the Evans are not afraid of whatever or whoever comes to call, life will go on as usual, unless something else happens. . .

Ghost Ship

The cold, dark, freshwaters surrounding the Bruce Peninsula have seen many shipwrecks. There are many unknown ships, their cargo and crew resting forever in the murky, silty depths. Some of the ships that have gone down have been sighted as "ghost" ships at different times throughout the years. Local history books say Jane Miller *is one of those ships whose final resting place has never been discovered, but whose ghostly image has been sighted from time to time.*

During one of the fiercest winter storms of 1881, a 78-foot wooden steam-powered propeller ship had left the port of Meaford with a heavy cargo, making her way through Georgian Bay along the Peninsula shoreline heading to Colpoy's Bay on her regular run. She had never had any difficulties that would warrant her being known as a problem ship.

Jane Miller, built at Little Current on Manitoulin Island, was a common sight to people who lived along the shoreline. They regularly saw the little steamer, built for duty, not beauty, chugging up and down the route between Meaford and Wiarton, going about her business of transporting goods and people up and down the Peninsula. As she was a steamer that burned wood instead of coal, much-needed deck and cargo space was taken up with piles of wood to use as fuel, and many more stops had to be made to replenish the wood necessary to heat her boilers. No permanent ballast was incorporated into the design of the ship, the wood being her ballast.

The heavy freight already loaded in Owen Sound had been added to after the steamer was re-routed to Meaford for a last-minute consignment of an additional thirty tons of freight. Most of the boxes, crates, and machinery parts were stowed on the deck, with the reason given that the captain wanted to load wood into the holds for her boiler. She was getting low and needed a refill, therefore *Jane Miller* must have already been top heavy when she left port. This fact escaped the captain and became more pronounced as time went on, and more and more of the wood ballast was used for fuel.

Though she rarely strayed more than half a mile from shore, the backtracking to Meaford for freight would have altered her course, making her travel across the exposed waters of Owen Sound, before coming into the relatively protected waters of Colpoy's Bay.

She was last seen west of Cameron Point by a man and his son, who heard a ship's whistle and looked out from their cabin onto the choppy waters at the entrance to Colpoy's Bay. They caught a glimpse of a vessel steaming into the southwest wind and waves, between the blinding gusts and gales of a snowstorm. They recognized the struggling ship as *Jane Miller*. The winter winds, snow, and ice would have added to the problem by making her list and become even more dangerously top heavy.

When the storm died down the next day, *Jane*

More Tales of the Unusual

Miller was long overdue at the Wiarton docks. Normally she ran on time and rarely experienced any real troubles. Family and friends gathered as searchers set out to try to locate the steamer.

No trace of the ship could be found. It was hoped that she had foundered on shore or had been blown off course somewhere. No such luck! Three men, searching for debris from the ill-fated steamer, reported seeing a strange bubbling, churning area of cloudy water lining up with Cameron Point. This was presumed to be the final, dismal resting place for *Jane Miller* and her 28 passengers and crew. Everyone on board would have been inside, protected from the fierce winter weather.

Later, a broken flag staff, oars, and five cloth caps, confirmed to have belonged to the crew of *Jane Miller,* were found washed up in a cove on White Cloud Island. Many times since the accident, the bottom of the bay has been dragged for traces of the steamer but with no success.

When Mother Nature works up her anger during a winter storm, a steamer like *Jane Miller* doesn't have a chance. She seemed to have disappeared into thin air! Some people speculate that due to the large cracks and crevices in the uneven bottom of the bay, *Jane Miller* may have broken up as she sank in the churning water during that terrible storm and washed into some deep, dark hole, never to be found, unless a scuba diver comes upon her during a trip into the cold waters of Colpoy's Bay.

Twenty years after the sinking of the steamer

More Tales of the Unusual

Jane Miller, there was a strange occurrence. A group of hunters, relaxing around their shoreline campfire one night, heard cries for help coming from somewhere out on the water. Not being able to do anything in the darkness, they had to wait anxiously for morning to come. Heading out in a boat in the daylight, they passed by an odd patch of coloured water bubbling up from the depths of the lake. There had been no storm to churn up the bottom. Looking around, they saw no boat nor debris—nothing to explain the cries for help or the strangely disturbed water.

When they reported the bizarre happening, they were told that possibly it was an echo, somehow carried down through time, of the desperate cries of the passengers and crew from the unlucky steamer *Jane Miller* trying to let her position be known.

Although she is still waiting, the little wooden steamer *Jane Miller* has not been forgotten. In 1968, the Ontario Department of Public Records and Archives placed a historical marker along Island View Drive (Grey County Road 26) near Wiarton to commemorate the loss.

High-Water Mark

Though it was some years ago, the strange happenings of a hot, humid day May 5, 1952, will be long remembered by people in the Stokes Bay area of the Bruce Peninsula. This story, told some years ago by the late Vincent Elliott, is definitely an unusual tale.

The day was quite warm for the time of year. Not a breath of air stirred the leaves, the Stokes River was gently meandering its way along, and a faint mist lay over the Bay. Mother Nature had given no clue as to what lay in store.

Breakfast was just over and the fishermen were getting ready to begin their day of work, mending nets or getting their boats ready for the upcoming fishing season. Some had their boats drawn up on shore for last-minute repairs, or tied to the government dock. The weather was fine, though there was the distant rumble of thunder.

Around eight o'clock that May morning, Mrs. McLay looked out the window and hurriedly called her husband Jack to come look outside; the garden was all covered with water. The river water had come up level with its banks and was now gently flowing across the road. This was the first seiche to arrive. A seiche is a wave that swings back and forth with a steady, uninterrupted rhythm, raising and lowering the level of water in lakes, bays, or rivers for periods lasting a few minutes or a few hours, usually as a result of seismic or atmospheric disturbances. Three different seiche tides came along that day, to interrupt the lives of the small community, each tide more violent than the one before.

No sooner were the village people aware that something strange was happening, than the tide went down. Vincent Elliott, at the shore getting ready to go fishing with a friend, stopped to take some photos, then headed off onto Stokes Bay, so he did not see things that happened later that morning, though he recounts experiences of friends and neighbours as told to him upon his return.

Just when things seemed to be all right again, the second, bigger tide came in about half an hour later, covering the road for some distance into the town. Becoming alarmed, some people put extra ropes on their boats to ensure their safety. This tide rushed away, leaving the river bottom almost dry and the fish gasping in the air. It was said that you could have walked across to Garden Island in your rubber boots. The Knife Island lighthouse boat was tied to a piling of the bridge and the son of the owner had to cut the ropes to prevent it from being dashed to pieces. He rode the boat downriver with the tide. His parents, farther out at the lighthouse in Stokes Bay, had not noticed anything out of the ordinary. Thinking that the worst must be over, no one had any inkling of what was to come.

The third tide, the "Big Seiche" to those who remember, came in just before noon. Again Mrs. McLay spotted the water. As the local postmistress, she was responsible for both the store and the Post Office which was beside the bridge. Because her family lived in back of the store, she regularly glanced out the window making sure that all was right with her world.

When the river started sneaking under the door, the mailbags and everything belonging to the Post Office must be moved. Neighbours in the next cottage came in to help and picked up a few things and put them on the table. By this time, the water was rising higher and higher so they took the cash box and money from the Post Office and went upstairs into the relative safety of the living quarters.

As Mrs. McLay and her friends looked out the window with horror at what was happening in their peaceful little village, they heard a bump noise from downstairs. The chesterfield was floating around the living room and the tin heater had risen up and disconnected from all its stovepipes, which came crashing down, raining black soot all over the room, mixing with the water and swishing a black soup throughout all the cupboards.

The neighbour woman started to cry when she saw her house move off its foundation and bob up and down in the water. Her heavy cook stove was the only thing that kept the little house from washing away.

There were people everywhere, evacuating their houses for higher ground, trying to carry what possessions they could. One man carried his wife on his back, and deposited her on dry ground. Dislodged woodpiles and lumber were swiftly floating along in the water. A wagon and a sleigh,

More Tales of the Unusual

stored behind a strong pole fence, floated up and went gliding over the top poles of the fence, down the road, and into the swamp. Boats, thought safely tied, broke free and went sailing off, some never to be seen again. Other cabins, of those less fortunate than Mrs. McLay's neighbour, were washed away into the swamp and wrecked.

The water rushed away as quickly as it had come, leaving devastation behind. Mrs. McLay's cat kept bringing her poor drowned kittens, one at a time, to the front doorstep. Fishing was easy that day, as many people filled baskets with stranded fish. The bridge was gone, vanished, leaving only pilings in its wake. Personal items were everywhere, soaked and many of them ruined. Shocked people, some still soaking wet, gathered in little groups, taking photos and discussing what had happened, though no explanation seemed forthcoming. No one had been hurt and that is what really mattered.

Mr. Elliott recounted that while all this was going on back in Stokes Bay village, he was out on the water fishing with his friend. A very heavy fog had come up. They could not see even a few feet away. Fishing was no good, though they were in a well-known deep hole; their line was acting strangely and it seemed to take off violently in one direction for no apparent reason. The fog lifted after about an hour or so and they were astonished. The two men found that they were not in Stokes Bay where they had started out, but had been carried along with the tide and were now in Gauley Bay, travelling so smoothly that they had not even noticed they were moving.

More Tales of the Unusual

Local townspeople were used to the ways of Lake Huron, knowing that there were "tides" of a sort. Water rose from an inch to a foot, depending on the time of year, and weather, especially before a storm. People were at a loss to explain the drastic change in the tide height that day in May. There was no wind and no storm in their area.

Mr. Elliott gave a possible explanation. He suggested that the tide could have been caused by an area of high pressure out over the lake, and that possibly Stokes Bay was in an area of extremely low pressure. This would have pushed a big mass of water into the Bay where it was magnified by the funnel shape of the Bay and the mouth of the Stokes River, like sloshing juice in a glass.

Who knows just what happened that day? We know, though, that it happened once, and it could happen again. Mother Nature has many surprises up her sleeve.

Jerry—Just a Lifeless Dummy?

Some believers think that inanimate objects can be haunted or possessed with the spirit of a previous owner, or that a wandering spirit may have taken up residence in the object. Such is the possible explanation of experiences with the wooden ventriloquist's dummy in the following story.

I interviewed a woman named Jodi, who worked at the Bruce County Museum & Archives as an outreach co-ordinator. Her job was to promote the Museum to the whole of Bruce County. She designed and set up rotating off-site exhibits at libraries, offered programs in towns all over Bruce County, and did special displays when requested. She was always looking for artifacts with great stories behind them. Jodi had a very interesting tale to tell.

The museum's public galleries consist of a two-storey schoolhouse built in 1878, and a single-storey exhibition hall added in 1975. On the grounds are a variety of outbuildings representing life in pioneer times. These smaller buildings are open seasonally, in the good weather.

When Jodi first came across Jerry, a ventriloquist's dummy, he was in an old wooden

More Tales of the Unusual

display case in the General Store Gallery of the Museum. His glass-sided case was an artifact itself. In it, he sat upon a little hand-carved child's chair, his wooden legs dangling and his painted eyes staring straight ahead. Clad in a time-worn homespun suit, he was an odd figure.

Jodi worked with Jerry on and off, occasionally taking him to off-site displays. He was intriguing and as his presence pricked her curiosity, Jodi began to research his origins at the Museum.

Jerry was a ventriloquist's puppet, hand carved by R.C. Pearce of Paisley. Mr. Pearce travelled all over Upper Canada entertaining people with his act. Travelling entertainers were very popular in centuries past. It was always a big event when they came to town. The story suggests that the ventriloquist originally had two puppets, Jerry and Joe. They supposedly looked alike, performed together and were stored together. Somewhere in the travels, Joe was lost, (stolen, states one story). He was never found.

In 1991, when researching and writing Jerry's story for *The Shoreline News,* October 29 edition, Jodi noted that Jerry was approximately 150 years old and had been residing at the Museum for 34 years.

Jerry's stay at the Museum began in 1957 when R.C. Pearce's granddaughter moved off her farm. She brought Jerry to the Museum, as a loan, to be put on display. At that time the Museum was just starting up and Women's Institute members were scouring the countryside looking for interesting donations and/or loans of artifacts.

More Tales of the Unusual

Jerry became a permanent part of the Museum's collection in 1981. That year, all the old donation records were examined and owners of artifacts on temporary loan, such as Jerry, were contacted and asked if they would donate the artifact to the Museum permanently. No member of the Pearce family wanted Jerry back, so at the Museum he stayed.

Although this is a relatively mild story when told in the light of day, things in the Museum seem to be very different at night, and some stories Museum staff told about the ventriloquist's dummy were chilling.

From time to time, Jerry reportedly was found in poses different from what he had been arranged in. One staff member told her that there had been a contract employee, (reputed to have some higher spiritual awareness), who refused to be in the same room as Jerry. She thought he was evil, possessed, an angry spirit. The stories were amusing and fun to recount to the students in the various museum programs, but did they have some underlying reality?

As for herself, Jodi liked Jerry, though his appearance was kind of spooky. His staring eyes and creepy, dried cornhusk hair were eerie. She could see why it wouldn't be appropriate to have him decorating the family living room.

One day, Jodi was in the General Store Gallery, getting ready for school programs. She and another staff member were recounting the stories about Jerry, tidying up the Gallery and getting the program materials ready for the next day. They left the Gallery, making sure everything was in its place and locked up.

Locking up the Museum is a bit spooky during any season, but this experience happened in late fall, when the darkness gathers its long shadows before five o'clock, making each day a bit more eerie as the season changes into the long nights of winter. Jodi didn't enjoy those nights when it was her turn to lock up.

Starting at the top of the old Public School building, closing all the gallery doors and turning off the lights, she would then go down to the next level and do the same thing. There were nights in the late fall and winter, when the urge to run from the old Public School building was overwhelming. The tiny sensitive hairs on the back of her neck would quiver with the sensation that there was something (or someone) behind her but when she would turn around, there was nothing there.

The urge to flee propelled staff quickly through the halls and down the stairs many nights. They eagerly left the building. Though she doesn't know for sure, Jodi doesn't remember locking up that particular night. She does remember walking in the semi-darkness to where she lived, just up the block from the Museum. It was a cold, wet November evening.

Later that same night the Museum's security company called around 9:30. They asked if she would come to let the police into the Museum. The alarm had gone off in the building and they needed someone to open the doors and to accompany the police through the Museum to check it out. In the dark, Jodi walked down the street where the shadows were long, the wind chilly and the sidewalks shiny with black puddles.

Jodi met the town police officer at the entrance to the Museum and unlocked the door. She ran in and checked the security system. The motion detectors had been set off in the General Store Gallery. The two searchers carefully wound their way through the dark halls of the Museum to check out the problem. The officer had a flashlight which he used to light the way. No sense turning on all the lights and alerting a possible intruder.

Jodi remembers her heart pounding with fright as they walked toward the Gallery. The Museum was as silent as an old building can be. There were the occasional creaks and groans as it settled itself but no other noise. No breaking glass, running footsteps, slamming doors. Just unsettling silence.

Making their way up the creaking steps to the Public School part of the Museum, they found no sign of disturbance. The gallery doors were all closed and the lights were off. After the lights in the General Store gallery were turned on and the door was opened, everything looked fine. The exits were checked and found to be locked with no sign of forced entry. Nothing appeared out of place.

As Jodi went back to shut the General Store Gallery doors, she noticed one thing. A small, seemingly insignificant thing. The door to Jerry's display case was open. He was still there, staring unsmilingly off into the distance; but his door was open. She was sure she had closed it when in the Gallery earlier that day. Had he just returned from a jaunt around the museum? Was he sitting in a slightly different position on the chair?

Puzzled, Jodi left it the way it was, closed the Gallery door and turned off the lights. As she walked through the Museum and locked it up again for the night, Jodi didn't say anything to the officer. It was just a stupid little detail, though it bothered her.

The next morning everyone talked in the staff room about the incident. Jodi had checked the Gallery again in the morning and the case was still open. The staff member she had been in the Gallery with was also sure the case had been closed when they left. They joked about Jerry, but deep down, Jodi wondered and still wonders if it is true that Jerry wanders, forever looking for his lost mate?

Do the night noises of the darkened Museum include the shuffle of leather-covered wooden feet?

A museum is a wonderful place with many artifacts that will take you back in time and tell you about your own history. Why don't you drop by and investigate for yourself? Jerry would be glad to see you I'm sure . . .

Justice Carried Out

Sometimes, a criminal had a bit of help from a higher power—which had absolutely nothing to do with his Maker . . .

In the days of long ago when justice was carried out much more swiftly than today, the crowd was judge, jury and executioner all in one. A person found guilty might have been seated on a horse, with the noose around his neck and attached to the tree before he could prove his innocence. Slap the horse and the deed was done!

Whether hung from a tree or from the wooden beam of the gallows, folklore tells us that if the trap door refused to swing open, even after re-tries, the person was thought to be innocent; if the rope broke while he was being hung, that also would prove his innocence. He might be "re-hung", but if the new rope broke, that was definite proof—the person was freed.

Because of the specific way the rope was twined and knotted, the "hangman's noose" was well known to do the job it was intended for. Therefore, if something went wrong, people believed a "higher power" must have intervened to show the error of the verdict.

Various local history books and newspapers tell us the story of John (Jack) Haag, a convicted criminal, found guilty of murdering a young man near

Formosa, who was sentenced to "hang by the neck until dead" in the exercise yard of the County of Bruce jail in Walkerton, Ontario. In years past, a large crowd usually showed up to watch a hanging. After all, it was entertainment to see someone get his just rewards.

The wooden scaffold and gallows, complete with strong uprights that held the rope and noose, had been constructed up high so the crowd could get a good view. After the charge was read out to the convicted criminal and to the crowd, the minister said a few last comforting words to the criminal. The hangman, usually an anonymous person brought in specially for the hanging, was hooded to protect his identity. He and the sheriff adjusted the noose one last time, then stepped back and sprung the trap of the gallows. The wooden floor dropped downward and the criminal was hung. Justice had been carried out.

Or had it?

Weeks later, while travelling through the U.S.A., the convicting judge at the trial of John Haag happened to see a man who looked surprisingly similar to the hanged man. Further investigation showed the "twin" to be the recently "deceased" John Haag. A conspiracy had been played out by his family which included the local sheriff, the jail doctor, the hangman himself and possibly a jail guard.

A special shoulder harness with a hook attached had been constructed to fit under the condemned man's armpits. This was placed beneath Haag's clothing and the hangman attached the noose to the hook. A second hook, hidden under Haag's long hair, kept the rope from tightening. After being hung and pronounced "dead" by the doctor, the convicted criminal was revived and hidden away until after a coffin of stones had been buried in his place, near "Glintz's Corner" in the cemetery along the Kincardine highway. As his family had "pull" he was not buried in unhallowed ground usually reserved for criminals or suicides. Sixty years or so later, the cemetery land was sold and the bodies were moved to the present Roman Catholic Cemetery.

There is no record whether the rotted remains of a wooden coffin surrounding only stones—not mortal remains—were found at that time.

Had it not been for the travels of the judge, the criminal and his entourage might have gotten away with this travesty of justice. But what finally became of Mr. Haag?

Light the Way

There were many shipwrecks in years gone by. Not all of them, however, could be attributed to Mother Nature. Sometimes, greed and underhandedness may also have played a part.

On November 24, 1872, as darkness descended, so too did another page in history. The 120-foot steamer *Mary Ward* was bound east from Owen Sound for Collingwood, Ontario. I researched various stories regarding the wreck of this ship. One blames the weather; another alleges alcohol use. Mechanical misuse or directional malfunctioning may have been involved. Whatever the cause, there were funerals for 14 people of the *Mary Ward*.

This 45-mile run was normally quite easy, but on this night, visibility was said to have been very poor. The lookouts were straining to see anything at all through the weather and the darkness. They were looking for the Nottawasaga Light with its lifesaving glow, to guide them into Collingwood. Thinking they were in position, and seeing a faint glimmer of light, the wheelsman and the captain agreed that the ship would swing starboard toward safety.

As the steamer headed closer and closer to land, the captain realized how wrong they had been. The glow they saw was from a lantern hanging at a boarding house at Craigleith, five miles short of Collingwood. With a grinding crunch, the steamer landed on Milligan's Reef three miles or so offshore. There she stayed.

The weather was still relatively calm and there was no reason for panic. Everyone was safe enough for now. Since the night was quite warm and the passengers and crew had nowhere to go, it was said that they relaxed and a festive air took over. Singing and music could be heard over the waters. Passengers stood on deck enjoying themselves. No one seemed to be at all worried.

The captain sent a small lifeboat to the shore at Craigleith. The men then would walk to Collingwood to get a tug, which they hoped could tow them off the reef so *Mary Ward* could continue up the shoreline to Collingwood. After contact was made, the 86-ton tug *Mary Ann* headed off toward the stranded steamer.

Shortly after midnight, while crew and passengers awaited the help of the tug, the weather took a decided turn for the worse. The wind came up and the clouds blocked out the stars. The whistle on *Mary Ward* began frantically blowing all hands on deck. Eight people launched another lifeboat and headed off for help. The yawl was hardly away, when it flipped in the waves and was sucked under the unforgiving, churning water.

The rescue tug *Mary Ann* arrived on the increasingly dangerous scene. She was helpless to assist those left on board *Mary Ward*. The rolling of the waves during the storm made the shoals too hazardous to go near. The tug could not get close enough to the ship. For her own safety, *Mary Ann* headed back to Collingwood.

The misery of those left behind on *Mary Ward* was unimaginable. In the rising intensity of the storm, the tug seemingly abandoning them was too much. Panicking, some of the men launched another boat, ignoring the cries from the other passengers.

Heading off into the storm was a futile attempt to save themselves. Mother Nature's fury took the men and the boat down to the cold depths of Georgian Bay. The men would have been better off staying with the grounded steamer. The approximately 24 people left on board *Mary Ward* survived the night and the ferociousness of the storm. The following day, the weather cleared and all aboard were rescued by the lighthouse keeper Captain George Collins and his son Charles from the Nottawasaga light, in their own boat, and by fishing tugs from Collingwood.

The vessel itself was a total loss. It is said that what was left of *Mary Ward* split apart and sank onto the limestone ledges that still bear her name, although some of the cargo and fittings were salvaged. Some of the cargo seemed to have disappeared into the hands of the locals. During the inquiry into the incident, it was claimed that the light hanging on a local boardinghouse was put there intentionally, by parties unknown, who hoped to ground a ship and steal her cargo. Though there was an investigation, this was never proven.

It is said that the spirits of those men drowned in the wreck of *Mary Ward* haunted the boardinghouse. The screech of the gulls is said to be the cries of those lost souls. The boardinghouse

More Tales of the Unusual

itself is long gone now, but the shoal where the wreck occurred is now known as the Mary Ward Ledges.

At Craigleith Provincial Park a plaque honours the memory of the victims of the *Mary Ward* disaster and the brave people who came to the rescue. For their courage, the Captain and his son each received $15.00 from the Canadian government. The wreck itself has been found and has become a popular dive site. Though difficult to locate, some remains are just beyond the second shoal north of Thornbury and Collingwood.

Sad to say, Charles Collins, unable to save himself as he had countless others over the years, drowned in 1872 while fishing on the Mary Ward Ledges.

Lingering Lavender

Strange events can happen anywhere. They are not just held to well-known historical spots. Memories—happy and sad—are said to sometimes remain with the area where they happened. Covering over the old with new doesn't always make a difference.

Making way for a new shopping mall, an old house was moved in 1985, from a site in Fergus, Ontario, to its present location near Mount Forest, replacing the old log home that had burned.

The frame house is a typical Depression-style home, nearly seventy years old. As there are no basements in most old houses, a new basement was built to accommodate the house, and a second floor was added. The frame house was not placed directly over the previous site of the log cabin, but moved about 30 yards north. What's left of the ruined timbers can still be seen. Usable leftover wood was made into storage sheds.

In 1989 a family rented a house 20 kilometres east of Mount Forest. Almost from the first day things started to happen. Unexplained occurrences began to make the family very uneasy.

The activities that took place usually happened in the afternoon, which was at that time the quietest art of the day. Rarely was anything felt at night. Like most animals, more sensitive than humans, the family dog hated to be in the house alone during the day but was usually fine when left alone after dark. This in itself was very unusual, especially where anything supernatural might be happening.

Activities centred around the kitchen and one downstairs bedroom in particular although, at times, a perfume smell seemed to drift throughout the whole house.

Funny things happened: toilet rolls were unwound; the phone cord tangled into a huge knot; pillows moved; the radio turned on and off. Most happenings were blamed on drafts from windows or the family pets, even old wiring, but the hardest to explain away was a powerful smell of lavender (which was a very popular scent used in the early 1900s) that seemed to drift around the rooms from time to time.

No matter what had happened, at no time did the family ever feel scared or upset by the activity happening around them. Noises were just presumed to be normal "old house" sounds. Visitors commented on the cosy, cheerful atmosphere of the home. Several times the children said they heard a whispery voice and what sounded like far-away singing, but the strangest thing of all happened late one night in the fall of 1993 as the family were preparing to move to a nearby property they had just purchased.

It was around one o'clock in the morning, when the parents were awakened by a loud noise coming from the kitchen. It sounded like grinding and the first thing they thought was the furnace was about to explode. Starting down the stairs, they were met by the family dog tearing upstairs at full gallop.

More Tales of the Unusual

When they reached the kitchen, they found all was quiet again. After a few minutes, the noise started again, making the parents jump into each other's arms. They realized the sound was coming from the electric can opener turning all by itself. They began to laugh at themselves for being so jumpy—until their eyes rested on the power cord. It was still lying on the counter top where it had been unplugged earlier in the day.

Quizzing the neighbours, the family learned a bit of the history of the original homestead site. As far as anyone knew no deaths had taken place in the ancient log house, but a couple of interesting stories about the immediate area turned up. The lot in question was originally part of a 100-acre farm, but was naturally severed as it is divided from the rest of the acreage by the South Saugeen River to the north, a drainage creek to the east and by two roads on the west and south. Around the turn of the nineteenth century, a log cabin was built as a retirement home for the old folks and the farm was willed equally to the surviving children, a son and daughter.

After the parents died, a disagreement caused the girl to move into the then-vacant cabin, while the boy continued to run the farm alone. This was around the 1920s. Though they continued to dwell on the same land, they lived totally separate lives, as though the other person did not exist. The siblings never even spoke to one another again.

The woman married and her husband was believed to have been killed in a logging accident in the area, sometime before World War II, only to be followed by her son in a similar accident several years later. She lived alone in the cabin until the 1960s when news came to her of the strange death of her brother.

He was walking in from the barn on a very stormy winter night and became disoriented in the blizzard. He was found two days later by a neighbour, frozen to death in the driveway of his house, just a few yards from his own front door, his frozen hand sticking up from a snow bank.

When the sister heard this news, neighbours say she must have become very distraught, possibly crazy with remorse. She went down to the river bank and drank a bottle of some sort of caustic solution, believed to be chlorine bleach. She too was dead by the time she was found.

Though the family now had a bit of understanding and explanation as to the history of the land, there was no real explanation for the strange happenings. As they had originally planned, they moved from the house shortly after that scary experience.

A few weeks after their move, the mother met the new tenant. When asked how she liked the place, the new resident said they loved the little house but they just wished they could get rid of the strong smell of lavender perfume. That family lived in the house for a year when they too had to move, supposedly because of a job transfer.

The next family who moved into the house lived there almost four years. They had a psychic friend visit them, who claimed there were several spirits present in the area of the river, but said she felt only one in the house, a very old lady.

There are new owners in the house again but so far they have not been asked their opinions.

How long will they last?

Time will tell!

Phantom Piper

This story comes to us through the folklore of Kincardine on Lake Huron. It is the romantic tale of a piper whose music of love for his family has continued down through the notes of time.

In 1856 many people were leaving their homelands to seek adventure or to better themselves from an otherwise bleak existence. The Sinclairs were just such a family. One bitterly cold winter an immigrant family from the Isle of Skye, Scotland, having uprooted themselves and travelled many, many miles over land and sea, found themselves on the last leg of their journey. The end was in sight. They had left the port of Goderich in a small vessel, heading for the shoreline of Penetangore (now Kincardine). They intended to farm the rich lands of Bruce County.

The October weather was overcast and as the boat approached Point Clark, the skies changed suddenly and a cold wind started to blow and chop at the waves, making the little boat bounce up and down in the dark, heavy waters. As daylight turned to dusk the captain feared that he would not find the shoreline safely in the dark.

The head of the family, Donald Sinclair, took up his pipes. He bowed his head and prayed for safe arrival and then played a powerful tune possibly trying to drown out the sound of the wind and weather and make his family feel more comfortable hearing the music of their homeland. Across the waters the music was heard by another piper in the town of Penetangore. He too took up his pipes and vigorously played music from the homeland in return. The skies cleared as suddenly as they had changed.

As the sun went down, the captain headed his vessel toward the sound of the bagpipes coming from the shoreline. All aboard arrived safely.

For many years after, Donald Sinclair often went down to the harbour to play the pipes at dusk, the rich melodies reminding him of his homeland. It was said that he did this to remember his narrow escape and good fortune, as well as to remind others of the power of the pipes.

During the summer months, if you visit Kincardine on a Saturday evening you will be regaled by the wonderful body-vibrating music of the bagpipes. Those who love the screel of the pipes can march behind the local pipe band and enjoy tunes that have been passed down from the Old Country.

The phantom piper has become symbolic of Kincardine, having been painted on the new water tower and appearing on brochures and advertising for the Scottish Festival happening each year.

Some evenings, at sunset, a piper plays from atop the Kincardine lighthouse to honour the memory of Donald Sinclair, as an early inhabitant of the shoreline town. His story has been passed down through the generations.

Who knows, if the vibrations are just right, you too may hear the rich lamentations of the bagpipes or see a shadowy silhouette gazing out over the water.

Poltergeist

There is a house just north of Paisley called the "Green House". This century home has been owned by the Green family for more than 10 years. Built in 1877, the dwelling has seen numerous owners and the various changes made by each. It seems that someone or something is not quite happy with those changes. This account appeared in The Beacon Times, *January 1996.*

Shortly after moving in, the Green family modernized the place slightly by rewiring the barn and several rooms in the house. Within six weeks strange, unexplainable occurrences started. Lights would turn off and on by themselves; the door bell would ring and no one would be there; the stereo would continue playing after it was turned off, and many other prankish incidents.

Then a most peculiar thing happened. The old cook stove in the kitchen had to be stoked up for the night before the last person went to bed. This was the main source of heat for the house and mornings were pretty cold. When trying to rekindle the fire one morning, the parents of the household noticed that something was not quite right. The fire would not light. Upon investigating, they found that the heavy stove had been moved four inches on its brick base and the stove pipe had been lifted up and out of the back of the stove.

More Tales of the Unusual

It took three hours to put everything back together as there was a gaping hole where the pipe should join the stove to the chimney pipes.

The sleeping family had not heard a sound and there had been no smoke billowing through the house that might have alerted them to any trouble. There was just no explainable reason for the pipes to come undone, or the stove to have moved. The heavy stove would require three or four people to move it.

Another time, the mother of the household was working in the barn doing chores, and was locked in a pen. There was no one else around the barn at the time and a child who was in the house came to check when her mother did not return for some time. She found the mother locked in the pen. The lock on the pen has to be manually operated and could not have latched itself accidentally.

In one of the upstairs bedrooms, a cousin of the family had a sensation of something coming up the side of the bed during the night. She won't stay in that bedroom again, but feels no fear staying in the house itself. The family dogs used to bark at one certain part of the kitchen for no apparent reason. Maybe there are multi-affected areas of the house. Ghost? Poltergeist? Nonsense?

It is said that when someone tries to take a photograph of the house in certain spots, the camera refuses to work. When the camera is turned away, it works just fine.

The family believes that something is causing these strange occurrences. Family members have tried to analyze all the events, but there is no forthcoming explanation. What could possibly start a tractor that had been rewired from a push-button-type ignition to a key ignition? What could move articles from their storage spots in the basement? Incidents have continued to accumulate and so have the unanswered questions. Logic rules out human activity, leaving the supernatural, for which there are no answers.

Although not frightened, the family never knows what to expect next. I'm sure they haven't heard the last of their invisible guest.

Prediction Fulfilled

Rural doctors, just as they are in the 21st century, were difficult to come by back in the 1800s. Training to become part of the medical profession was hard work. Life was tough. Employment and money were short and death was waiting just around the corner.

As I was visiting the Grey County-Owen Sound Museum one day, I happened to notice a rich, deep almost blood-red, very ornate wooden carving sitting in the front entranceway to the main museum gallery. It is quite large, standing about 5 feet tall. I inquired about it and was given a write-up telling the tale of its arrival at the museum. I did some further research and came up with a strange, rather mixed-up story surrounding the carving ...

Because there is very little written about the life of Edward Henry Horsey, one gathers that his family life unravelled rather normally until he grew up, finished school and headed off into the future of his manhood. Practising medicine for only a short time, Dr. Horsey grew to dislike the career he had probably looked upon as being his life's work. Looking to make a dramatic change, he left the town of Owen Sound and travelled to the far-off reaches of the mysterious Orient, where his life was about as different to what he had, as it could get.

More Tales of the Unusual

There, after just a short time spent adjusting to the strange ways of his new home and being a knowledgeable man, he started work as an executive of the Sun Life Insurance Company.

His life again must have gone on somewhat normally and, after working up the corporate ladder of success, he returned to his roots in Owen Sound some years later, a prosperous man. By 1900 he had become quite well known in the community and was elected as North Grey's representative in Parliament. He also had a good job working at the Sun Portland Cement Company in Owen Sound, a thriving part of the business community. Life was good!

In 1902, while he was showing a company director around the cement plant, something unexplainable happened. An engine flywheel from a piece of machinery burst apart, causing serious damage to the building.

It was a miracle that Dr. Horsey's business companions were not injured in the strange accident, considering the extensive damage to the structure. But alas, the young doctor, who had come such a long way in such a short time, died as a result of a machine fragment penetrating his head.

A strange follow-up to the doctor's death occurred as his estate was being closed up, and his worldly goods disposed of. An ornate, strangely carved wooden statue of what looked like some sort of Oriental deity was found amongst his possessions. It was obviously hand carved and was of a deep, dark, blood-red colour.

A peculiar prediction came to light when

someone remembered that when the doctor received the odd sculpture as a gift in China, it had been predicted that just such an unhappy ending should come to the person who removed it from its place of rest far, far away on the other side of the world. Obviously the late Edward Horsey did not believe in predictions. Too bad that he didn't heed the warning.

The wooden statue has been donated to the Grey-Owen Sound Museum and is on display in their main museum building.

Research suggests that the carving depicts one of the Eight Immortals of Taoism who lived during the Mongol dynasty—possibly Li-Tie-guai (spelling varies)—reborn as a beggar, crippled in one leg and using a crutch. He is holding a gourd which myth says contained a substance that could miraculously restore life to the dead.

Rest in Peace

Owen Sound, Ontario, has some old buildings that seem just ripe for haunting. The former county courthouse, on 3rd Avenue East, one of Owen Sound's earliest buildings, may have some residents who have no reason to leave. There have been many unexplainable happenings. The age of the building itself, not to mention the Hangman's Yard, or the resulting burials on the property are enough to give rise to scary images.

The old stone courthouse building, which at one time was the place where a criminal could be tried, sentenced and the punishment carried out, has not been used for any sort of judicial business since the construction of a new one in 1960. The building has been renovated into separate offices. The Georgian Bay Folk Society used some of the space and other rooms were rented by artists and various businesses.

Over the years unexplainable things have been happening. An artist, working late into the night and then on into the early morning, was in his studio on the second floor. He heard the heavy tread of someone walking up the nearby steps. He also heard the mumble of a voice and thinking it was a male, his first thought was that it was a friend coming to see him.

His second thought was to remember that he

was alone in the building and that the doors had been locked.

Still expecting to see someone—anyone—he opened the door to nothing! There was no one. The hair on his body became as though electrically charged. It stood on end when, after opening the door, a slight wind gave him the feeling of the presence of something. He also smelled a strong odour, skunky, but not as strong as fresh skunk.

Confused, he closed the door. He tried to brush off what had just happened, but upon opening the door again, just to check, he had the same experience. He abruptly left the building.

When he works in the building now, he always has the sensation that somebody is behind him. He does not have that feeling in any other building.

Unless he has someone with him, the artist no longer works late into the night.

A previous tenant of the same office space, a photographer, had a strange experience as well, while he occupied that area. He too was working late into the night. He estimated that it was around midnight or half-past twelve. Suddenly, seeming to come from nowhere, he heard a male voice say, "Hi!"

The voice seemed to be just a few feet away, but looking wildly around him, the photographer could see nothing. Getting up quickly, he looked into the nearby old courtroom, again seeing nothing. There was no sound either of footsteps coming or going. He went out into the hall, but again, saw nothing. His frantic brain finally concluded that there was nobody (live) around. At no time did he feel any sense of danger toward himself. Thoroughly "spooked" though, he left the building shortly after.

The photographer never had another experience like that one, although it is constantly in the back of his mind when he enters the building. The hairs on the back of his neck rise with the fear and anticipation of something happening.

Another client in the building, who was also working late one night, also alone, heard what he thought were male footsteps down the back stairs. He then heard what sounded like a sack being dragged across the floor. A search along the hallways and other offices revealed nothing. Stopping back in his room only long enough to grab his keys, he left the building.

The old courthouse itself has probably seen many colourful characters in its time. A variety of criminal offenses were judged in the old courtroom. Not all the criminals were given jail time. Sentences of hanging were carried out in the Hangman's Yard. The wooden gallows were placed right next to the courthouse, in the southeastern corner, where a high fence blocked the view of sightseers. Local stories say that at least a few people were buried in the jail yard.

Is someone haunting the old courthouse? Who knows. It could be the ghost of Cook Teets, who met his death at the end of a hangman's noose, protesting his innocence until the very end. His death, December 5, 1884, at age 55, viewed by those with invitation only, has the unfortunate point in history of being the first execution to take place in Owen Sound.

More Tales of the Unusual

The well-respected Teets family, originally from upstate New York, were among the earliest settlers in Artemesia Township, and helped open the land of the Queen's Bush. After establishing a fine farm, they built and operated a sawmill and furniture factory. Cook Teets was blinded by a snowball as a child. He married later in life, to a considerably younger woman. Nothing in Cook Teets' background suggested he would die a violent death, at the end of a rope, judged a murderer.

After the sudden death of his wife, Rosannah, at the home of her parents, a doctor from Flesherton had the contents of the victim's stomach sent to Toronto for analysis. The tests showed that Rosannah Teets had died as a result of strychnine poisoning.

Although the evidence was largely circumstantial, Cook Teets was charged in the death of his young wife. The short-lived marriage seemed to be stormy from the beginning. As the beneficiary of a recently issued insurance policy on Rosannah, Cook Teets' future looked even dimmer after the finding of strychnine poison in a shed on the farm.

Acknowledging that he had the poison, he told the court that he had given his mother-in-law some of it to help rid her of dogs bothering the cattle. Also, telling of the controlling hand the family had upon Rosannah herself and then finally the death of his wife at their home, Teets loudly protested his innocence.

Though there was no direct evidence proving his guilt, Cook Teets was found guilty and sentenced to die. Carpenters got to work and the sturdy wooden gallows were erected in the jail yard. Fifty to sixty people gathered in the early hours just after dawn one cold winter morning, to see the hanging take place. Proclaiming his innocence to God, Teets announced he would die with a clear conscience. Moments later he was dead.

At precisely eight o'clock, the black flag was run up the courthouse flag pole to tell of the death of Cook Teets. Many church bells tolled their sombre notes. He was buried in the city cemetery, though he may not be resting quietly. . . .

School Section #10

Schools are some of the most well-known hot spots for supernatural happenings. Over the years, with all the different types of children attending, schools seem to become highly charged emotional sponges. Possibly, from time to time, some of the pent-up emotions need an outlet.

Built in 1862, the wooden schoolhouse served its small community well, as school, church, and meeting place. It was assigned the simple name S.S. #10, Glenelg Township, in the rural area near Durham, Ontario. S. S. stood for School Section, identifying the area from whose taxes the school was supported, and whose children attended the school.

Most of the inhabitants were immigrants, simple folk who uprooted their families, journeying from the Old Country to a better life in Canada. Many had travelled from Ireland and Scotland, bringing their beliefs and customs with them. Belief in the supernatural was commonplace amongst the early settlers of Grey and Bruce counties. What better to make themselves feel at home than tradition, so it was not so far-fetched or scary that something unusual would happen in the little wooden schoolhouse, that warm spring day, May 21 of 1894.

The little building probably looked like the usual pioneer schoolhouse. On a clearing of land donated by a local landowner, the school would have been built by the locals with donated materials. Some trees and possibly a couple of swings stood in the yard. Out back was the privy, shared by both boys and girls. The wood pile stood by the side of the school, waiting to fill the wood stove, keeping the room warm in the spring, hot and steamy in the winter. Cedar rails or possibly a weather-worn picket fence would travel around the perimeter of the schoolyard, keeping students in and cattle out. The teacher stood on the stoop, arm pumping, ringing the bell to call the children to class.

More than thirty years passed, students and teachers coming and going over the years. Life went on pretty regularly until that particular spring. The school day started normally. It was now nearing lunch time and growly tummies make restless children.

The schoolmarm, noticing an irritating humming or groaning sound coming from somewhere in the room, left her podium to search it out. She wandered among the students, eagerly working their way through the schoolwork, toward lunch time and freedom. The noise was not heard by the students and seemed to move around the room with her as she searched it out. Not being able to pinpoint where the sound was coming from, as the teacher later explained to reporters, she thought the noise the result of an unshakable, week-long headache.

Lunch time came and went. Afternoon classes started as usual. Or, not so usual... the noise was there again, moaning and groaning its way through until the end of the day. Putting it down to the wind, the teacher dismissed it from her mind.

More Tales of the Unusual

Tuesday, May 22, 1894, should have been just another school day, except the irritating moaning groaning was still there. The volume of the noise had magnified into a roar that nearly drowned out the teacher. The children heard the noise now. Not being able to teach, the schoolmarm dismissed her students after only an hour. The children went home to tell their parents and the teacher promptly informed the chairman of the school trustees.

Wednesday, May 23, 1894, showed a procession of students, school trustees, and the teacher arriving together at S.S.#10. The groaning humming noise began in earnest, rising and falling in volume. The trustees were convinced that the teacher and her students were working together to have some fun at their expense. After intense searching and testing of the building, the trustees failed to discover the source of the strange noises. The students were again dismissed from class for the day.

Thursday, May 24, was a holiday, to celebrate the queen's birthday. The school trustees met again at school that day. Strangely, though there were no students, there also were no unusual noises.

Friday's school day dawned as usual. In school only 15 minutes, class was again dismissed because of the strange noises.

Saturday and Sunday brought out a group of concerned parents, trustees, and community members. Children were not allowed in the area. Silence reigned.

Monday morning brought the start of class. The trustees stood at the back of the schoolroom. Again, the throbbing humming began. Frustrated, the teacher demanded that the noise stop immediately. An adamant reply came forth from somewhere in the room, "No, I won't!"

To make a long story short, adult men replaced the children one day. The noise did not abate. It seemed to come from everywhere and nowhere at the same time. Ventriloquism was suggested, but rejected. The school was searched with a fine-toothed comb. Nothing could be found to explain the mysteries of the last few days. Local newspapers were selling plenty of copies that week.

Moving the students and teacher to a temporary school in a nearby church did not stop the moaning and groaning in the original schoolhouse. Crowds of onlookers visited the school and were treated to an auditory display of the supernatural. So explained, because there simply was no explanation. The school had been examined from the rafters to the dirt floor and nothing strange was observed.

Suddenly as they had begun, the strange noises stopped. The trustees in their hopeful eagerness ordered classes back to the little wooden schoolhouse. Tentatively, the teacher began her lessons. The children were as nervous at starting class as she was. Under watchful eyes, the day progressed until it was dismissal time. Nothing unusual had happened. That was the end of the moaning, groaning, humming noises. No explanation was ever found.

Many theories were given over the next little while as to the cause for the noises. Some blamed the damp weather for swelling the wood, making

More Tales of the Unusual

unexplained noises; others suggested hollows under the ground filling with water and the air venting through the schoolhouse and so on. Though the noise had stopped, the "ghost" still caused great excitement and talk in the village.

School finished in June. In late fall a new school, complete with a new teacher, began a new term. Some students tried to start another obvious "ghost" to no avail. Life returned to normal and practical jokers were dealt with. There was nothing supernatural about the new Glenelg school.

The old wooden schoolhouse became the property of a local farmer who moved it to his land to use as a drive shed. Nothing strange there. Did the "ghost" move on to a new residence?

Tarred and Feathered

In days gone by, crime on the high seas—real or imagined—was dealt with swiftly and usually painfully. There was no trial by jury, and the victim was not presumed innocent until proven guilty, as in today's judicial system. Walking the plank as in pirate lore was not a common occurrence. Punishment was usually handed out by those presuming themselves to have been offended against, and by their followers. Whipping, or tarring and feathering seem to have been the usual punishment.

The mysterious and tragic death of a young Purple Valley boy many years ago, while working as a deck hand on the steamer *Baltic*, created such a furor that newspapers from as far away as Toronto and London called it "The Baltic Case". This story was even included in the book, *Memoirs of a Great Detective, incidents in the life of John Wilson Murray,* written in 1904, the detective having been involved in the dramatic case.

A young man in September 1889, fresh off the farm near Wiarton, Charlie Hambly put his belongings in a sack, slung them over his shoulder and set off for the life of a sailor. He had lived near Colpoy's Bay his whole life, watching the coming and goings of ships and their crews from his family home high on the shores of Georgian Bay. Charlie's grandfather had carved wooden ships for him from the time he was a young child, and had taught him to sail them on the streams. Having a great love for the water, Charlie longed to be a sailor and see the world. So, after saying good-bye to his parents, he set off on what was to be a tragically short journey.

With no ship experience, but dreaming of life on the sea, young Charlie took his kit and made his way to the bustling port of Owen Sound. He proudly signed up to be a deck hand on the steamer *Baltic*, which sailed the waters between Owen Sound and Sault Ste. Marie. There were about 20 people working on the steamer, as well as some paying passengers. Learning of Charlie's lack of sailing experience, and his attitudes toward temperance, some of the crew set about to test and tempt Charlie with illegal drink. The hard-living, hard-drinking, rough semi-literate crewmen hassled Charlie constantly. They saw him as looking down his nose at them. More and more, the crew saw Charlie as a troublemaker or goody-goody.

Rumours of Charlie's observing the crew stealing alcohol from the cargo may have been one supposed explanation for the tragedy about to follow. Although there were witnesses to the actual acts who came forth in court later, no one was sure, nor offered the truth as to the trigger for the fair-haired boy's punishment. A proud member of the Wiarton Sons of Temperance Lodge, Charlie had never touched a drop of alcohol, and probably did not look favourably on those who did. These ideals did not bode well for Charlie.

Whatever the excuse, young Charlie was hunted down like a rabid dog, roughly seized and plunked down in the centre of the circle of angry, drunken men. He was ordered to drink, but refused. Holding him, the men tried to force the liquor down his throat. Clenching his jaws so they could not be forced open, Charlie endured being spat upon, kicked, and otherwise abused. Breaking away from his tormentors, he ran. The drunken crewmen again hunted down the frightened boy.

Spied in his hiding place, Charlie was dragged out onto the moonlit deck. The crew, their hatred building, decided to tar and feather the boy. Two crewmen went for the tar while another slit open a feather pillow. Holding Charlie down, others stripped him of his clothes and beat him.

Struggling, probably frightened for his life by now, the boy was covered in tar and feathers, and beaten with a paddle. He was paraded around the deck for all, crew and passengers alike, to see. With Charlie crying and begging for mercy, the captain appeared on deck. Going along with some alleged offence against the boy, he ordered the anguished Charlie to pack his bags, as he would be leaving ship at the next port of call.

All hope extinguished, no reprieve from his torture forthcoming, Charlie was in shock and sobbing, pleading to be understood and saved. Chased again, Charlie tried to escape his abusers. He gave a soul-wrenching scream, so a witness later told the inquest jury, and leaped over the side of the ship into the cold, dark waters of Georgian Bay. He was never seen again.

At the next port, police were called upon to check out the story of some dismayed passengers.

More Tales of the Unusual

Drunken bragging by some of the guilty parties, and eyewitness accounts led to six arrests and charges of manslaughter, and trial by judge and jury. Four of the crew were sent to prison. The captain's license was suspended for a year for his part in the dastardly deed. He did not even have the humanity to stop the ship or order a lifeboat to be lowered, to see whether Charlie could be saved. He had been heard publicly to threaten the life or ruin of any person who gave witness against him.

In spite of the threats, witnesses did testify. The jury brought in a guilty verdict, although the length of the sentences did not compensate for the murder of an innocent farm boy. Charlie's body was never recovered, and the reason for his murder is still talked of in the Hambly family.

One of the writeups regarding the murder and subsequent trial had this strange ending to the tale. The writer went to the Hamblys' house to ask when they last heard from the boy. They told him that they had received Charlie's note about shipping off as a sailor. As the father had taken out the letter to read for about the hundredth time, he thought he heard a cry in the night. The old man thought he heard Charlie calling out. He opened the door and stepped outside to listen. He knew he must have been mistaken, for how could he have heard Charlie, even if his son had called? How right he was!

The Crying Boy

It is said that living beings have an aura surrounding them, that is the colour of the flow of life that makes that person or animal what it is. The aura can be a dark colour for a dark, moody person, but light and vibrant for a happy, contented person. The aura is not seen by most people but rather felt by them. You can tell when you are with a happy person, or entering a happy home. Some art seems to have a feeling about it as well. A painting takes on part of the artist who made it.

In the shoreline village of Oliphant on the Bruce Peninsula, an oil painting crafted by an artist long dead hangs on the living room wall of a residence. The painting is known to the family as "The Crying Boy", and has been known by that title forever. The main focus of the painting seems to be the eyes, which are blue. They seem able to be seen from anywhere in the room, and they follow you around anywhere in the room. Did the artist who originally painted it have a wonderful talent or . . .is it something else?

About 19 inches by 27 inches, the painting shows a young, brown-haired boy, eight or nine years of age. It is only his mid-chest and up that is represented. He has a slightly sad face, with a single tear on his right cheek, his lower lip gently pouting.

He wears a dark, fisherman's-knit sweater. Originally coming from Holland, the painting has been in the family for at least six generations that they can remember.

Presently the painting has a backing of particleboard. Originally, it was framed with a real wood frame, but after surviving various fires, the canvas was mounted without a frame. Therefore, we cannot tell whether there is any writing on the back of the canvas. The fire that did the damage to the frame also burnt the back of the canvas but, mysteriously, the painting itself survived intact.

The current owner of the painting is the youngest son in the family. The painting was passed down to him after his maternal grandfather died several years ago. Now owning the painting, he placed it in the same location in his home as it had been in his grandfather's house, with a photograph of his grandfather beside it.

Even though you now have a bit of the background, there is nothing to explain the strangeness that surrounds the painting, something about it related to fire. No one can remember how the story goes. Each of the owners of the painting has suffered some sort of fire or fires, the last in 1999.

After the flames were extinguished, and the firefighters had departed, the homeowner was allowed to salvage what he could from the home. While the house itself was almost a total write-off, the painting survived! The wall behind the painting was blackened and charred, the wallpaper burnt, and the surrounding photographs ruined beyond recognition. Even the photograph of the grandfather, placed right beside "The Crying Boy" was destroyed.

Though not burned, the boy had a slight hazy, smoky wreath encircling his face. The glow of his face shone eerily through the dirt, his eyes still seeming to follow people anywhere they might move in the room.

The painting is back on the wall, though the house is still being rebuilt and renovated after the fire. No matter where you are in the room, or what you are doing, your eyes always travel back to the painting, to glance at it, to stare at it. It stares right back at you as if it were alive.

Generations ago, itinerant artists rendered paintings of families in return for room and board and some monetary compensation. Some paintings were done after a family member had died, even with the body still in the room, as there were no cameras to take photographs then. Many of these travelling artists were unknown. The signature on the painting looks like *T. Braaglin.*

Not knowing who the child is makes the reason for the survival of the painting through many fires all the more mysterious. Possibly, in this painting, there is more than just the aura of the artist. Perhaps the child is protecting himself still, many, many years after his death.

The Curse

Much of our Canadian folklore begins with a slight stretch of the truth. Over time, the truth is embellished slightly and some drama added here and there. Before you know it, you have a "true" story.

This tale comes from Elsinore, Ontario, which lies northeast of Southampton and just down the road from Allenford. There are no ruins left of the farmhouse which once stood on the site just off Concession 13, Arran Township. In this place a terrible curse was uttered—a curse that some people swear came true!

This story is a memory, recorded in the Bruce County Historical Society Yearbook 1996. *In these yearbooks are wonderful stories, bits and pieces of the past which otherwise might be forgotten. Though there is nothing to show that a home ever existed on the property as the bush has been let grow almost right out to the road, some believe that the story of the curse is true. You can decided for yourself. . .*

Our storyteller, Mr. L. Hunt, remembers back to the early 1930s, when, early on Christmas Day, his family had finished the chores and were getting ready to go celebrate at the home of their grandparents at Chesley Lake. Being only ten years old, he was looking forward to all the excitement of

More Tales of the Unusual

Christmas: the goodies, the presents, and everything else that was part of the holidays. He also remembered something his mother said on their way out to dinner, when passing the ruins of an old homestead. It had snowed quite heavily during dinner, and afterward, on their way home again, their old Chevy got stuck in the snow. As they shovelled the car free, the boy asked his father to explain what Mother meant about the curse, she having stayed behind with his sister to do more visiting.

The father started his strange story by telling him that back around the turn of the century (1900 or so to those in the new millennium), a crippled old man—known then as a hunchback—lived in relative isolation on his farm. He was very sensitive about his condition, coming out only when necessary. This made him known to his neighbours as something of a recluse, and thus he was deemed eccentric as he was not out and about keeping up with the times.

During some of his visits to town, he became the subject of cruel jokes; the boys in the neighbourhood played many pranks on him. One of the boys happened to draw a chalk diagram of the hunchback on the side of the house. It was a hideous depiction that emphasized his painful condition. The old man was furious.

It was said that he uttered a curse upon the boy. Loudly, the man exclaimed, "The hand that drew that picture shall come off, and the person who drew that picture shall have an offspring that is more seriously crippled than I am." Though it became the talk of the town, after a while the excitement died down and no one thought much of the prediction. Time went on.

More Tales of the Unusual

Supposedly the curse did come true. Some say, while still a young man, the boy who had made the chalk drawing was working in a sawmill. He lost a hand and wrist to the whirling blades. The rest of the curse was also fulfilled when the young man's wife gave birth to a disfigured child.

Did a "curse" really come true, or were tragic circumstances explained as the results of a curse?

Unidentified Flying Object

In my first book, you will have read that Bruce and Grey counties seem to have been busy places for UFO sightings in the late 1970s and early 1980s. Many people recall seeing weird objects in the night sky. If you lie in the fields in the black of night, you can still see unusual and unexplainable objects darting through the dark skies above. You know these quickly moving objects are not stars, nor the precisely orbiting satellites of our modern-day media world. They are Unidentified Flying Objects, for which, as yet there is no explanation!

Leaving Wiarton, a local resident was on her way home from work. She had picked up a few groceries as she regularly did. It was around nine o'clock on a cold, crisp, clear February night about 1990. When she turned off Highway 6 at Clavering and headed toward Sauble Beach, the woman was startled to see ahead of her a large circle of light hanging in the dark sky. She didn't know what it was, but it was not the moon. She thought it looked very close to her house so, pushing the gas pedal harder, she rushed up the road. She remembers feeling very scared.

As she drove in a panic closer and closer to her house, she realized that the bright object was actually two concessions away. She screeched into the driveway, gravel flying. She pushed the door open, almost falling out of the car, and then ran into the house. The shaking woman dragged her husband outside, still in his slippers, to see the sight.

They both stood shivering in the middle of the road, looking toward the Sauble Beach area. Pointing to it confusedly, they wondered out loud what the object was. Her husband said a plane, but his wife noticed no movement or engine sound. He thought of a helicopter, but they heard no engine, only the silence of the cold night broken by the crisp snapping of twigs and branches.

Finding no explainable answer, the husband, relatively undisturbed by what he had seen, went back into the house, with his scared wife following closely on his heels. Looking back again, she saw that the UFO had vanished. In the house, the woman still felt so scared she would not even stay downstairs by herself at the time.

Later in the week, while talking to neighbours who lived farther north along the road, she told them of her experience. Others said that they had seen the sight that night as well. Apparently unexplainable lights had shone in the night sky in other nearby areas. Someone had inquired about the army base at Meaford, which does night manoeuvres with flares but, as the base is in the opposite direction, near Georgian Bay, nothing would come over Lake Huron way. No answer there. There have been no explanations of those lights to date, but the woman remembers the night as if it were yesterday. Now, she is much more aware of what goes on in the night skies.

Underwater Wonders

Scuba diving is an exciting sport made more popular by the ease of travelling around the world, and the many television programs showing the wonders to be found underwater. There are also many unusual objects to be found. Some are man-made, some are natural. All over Earth's waters, plotting and graphing continually updates marine charts. Some strange things seen underwater justify further investigation. Located in the cold depths of Colpoy's Bay, near Wiarton, Ontario, is the remains of an ancient forest. Farther north, off Tobermory, is yet another ancient underwater wonder.

In 1977, while enjoying the waters of Colpoy's Bay from underneath the surface, scuba diver Al Given of Wiarton made a startling discovery. In an area well known for its sunken ships, Mother Nature herself had a surprise for the well-seasoned diver. Ahead of him in the murky depths were the remains of an underwater forest.

As exciting as this discovery was, he did not think much of his find again until 1993. Al runs a small dive shop in Wiarton and was always talking of his finds to divers renting his equipment. He enjoyed diving and decided to visit the underwater forest site again on one of his trips. This forest, accessible only by boat and scuba equipment, lies in about 34 feet of very cold water, on the northwest side of Gunderson Shoal, northeast of Wiarton. The forest, with its top vegetation long since rotted away, now consists only of ragged tree stumps sticking out of the silty, sandy bottom of the bay.

Knowing he had made a significant discovery, Al sawed off some samples of the wood and sent them to botanists to be tested. Carbon testing on the Georgian Bay cedar stumps dated the wood between 4,500 and 7,600 years old.

Studies of the tree rings showing growth patterns concluded that the underwater cedars grew at least as slowly as today's cedars above water level. This shows that the moisture and drought patterns have not changed greatly over time. The water levels in the past were much lower that they are now; over the years, rising waters covered the lower forests.

The oldest living cedar found along Georgian Bay so far is 1,550 years old. With others of the same species, it survives in craggy outcroppings along the face of the limestone cliffs on the Bruce Peninsula. These trees can be reached only by rappelling down the rocks.

Divers have discovered underwater forests in at least three other areas in the waters off the Bruce Peninsula. One is adjacent to, and a bit south of Cyprus Lake, in depths from 40 feet to 60 feet. Another is at Johnston Harbour on the Lake Huron side of the Peninsula, just south of Tobermory. The third is just off Cape Croker, Chippewas of Nawash First Nation, on the Georgian Bay side.

Like the trees, landforms are constantly affected

More Tales of the Unusual

by changes in weather and climate. Ice Ages carved lakes and rivers, melting waters filled them, and hills formed in the wake of the glaciers, while earthquakes raised and lowered land.

At the tip of Tobermory, the land seems to end. To proceed by car, you must take the ferry across to South Baymouth. Underwater, out of sight, lies the continuation of the limestone cliffed regions of the Niagara Escarpment, jutting here and there out of the water, then submerging again. These waters require cautious boating. It has been suggested that at one time the peninsula extended all the way across to Manitoulin. Interesting geology, as well as the very cold water temperatures and sudden depths, make for exciting, possibly dangerous scuba diving. All these factors must be taken into consideration when choosing safe diving sites in Fathom Five National Marine Park.

Four people died in 1965 seeking one special geological site.

In 1994, the Canadian Forces ship, *Cormorant,* was working on a study of the Great Lakes using sonar and other scanning equipment. Between Flowerpot Island and Dunk's Point to the east, the crew discovered something wonderful. Rising up from the floor of the bay, about 100 feet below the surface, what appeared to be an underwater waterfall came into view on their screens. Described as a post-glacial waterfall, it is 40 to 80 feet from top to bottom, and from 3,000 to 3,600 feet across. It would not easily be recognizable as a waterfall, because we are used to seeing this feature on the surface of the land.

More Tales of the Unusual

This waterfall would have been above water approximately ten thousand years ago, when our water levels were much lower than they are today. In the distant past when the Niagara Escarpment itself was entirely above water, the waterfall would have brought the cold waters of Lake Huron into the smaller Georgian Bay. Its size and strength must have competed with the falls we call Niagara.

We can only imagine how beautiful and majestic it looked.

Where's Mom?

"Living the quiet life" in the country does not automatically mean there are no problems such as those associated with big cities. In is just that these memorable events happen less often where everybody knows everybody, and therefore stay in people's minds longer. This particular story appears in a local history book and other short-story crime books.

An event that lives on in the annals of crime-fighting and lawyers' archives, it is known as the first murder tried in Canada for which the criminal was charged without the benefit of a body as proof of the crime. This sensational murder trial focused national attention on the small community of St. Edmunds Township. It was known as The Kendall Murder.

In the early 1950s the Bruce Peninsula was not highly populated. A great influx of people came during the summer, with most of them leaving when the weather got cooler. Others, liking the supposedly idyllic life of the country decided to stay. A Mr. Arthur Kendall came to the Bruce Peninsula on an early springtime fishing trip, and liked the area so much that he accepted a job at a sawmill at Johnston Harbour. Knowing he had a family and a farm to run at Monkton, Ontario, he decided to stay for the summer anyway.

One day, out of the blue, he asked his family to

join him at the beginning of summer. Unknown to his wife and children, in the time that Arthur Kendall had been staying in the Bruce, he had developed an intimate relationship with one of the local women who worked in a Wiarton restaurant.

The Kendall family arrived, lock, stock, and barrel, and took up residence together once again. Nothing unusual happened within the family until August 2, 1952. On that day, Helen, the wife of Arthur Kendall and mother of five children disappeared. On the same day, Arthur Kendall abruptly gathered all of his possessions and the five children and left the area. He left a note for his employer saying that he would not be back to work due to family problems.

Driving through Wiarton, stopping only to pick up his lover and her six children, the Kendall family, as crowded and uncomfortable as it must have been, drove to the original family farm at Monkton.

There, neighbours noticed the reappearance of the Kendall family, and inquired as to the whereabouts of Helen. They also noticed the new woman and the additional children. Arthur Kendall explained that Helen had deserted the family. A week later, the same neighbour visited, and inquired after Helen. Kendall told him that Helen was with her mother. The neighbour went home and phoned Helen's mother, who informed him that Helen had not been to see her, or called either, in quite some time.

Alarmed at the inconsistent answers, the neighbour called and reported Helen's absence to the Ontario Provincial Police. Helen's brother, after hearing from his mother about the disturbing telephone call from the Kendalls' neighbour, drove out to the Kendall farm to ask about Helen. He too was unconvinced by Arthur Kendall's answers and notified the OPP.

The police investigation began the next day, August 12, 1952. Arthur Kendall's statement and those of the children matched exactly. They did not match anything told to the OPP by the witnesses who had inquired after Helen. Although the area around Johnston Harbour was searched extensively and many people were questioned, Helen's body was never found. No other incriminating evidence was uncovered to suggest foul play; therefore, Arthur Kendall was not charged.

In 1960, Helen Kendall was declared legally dead. Arthur Kendall and his lover were married.

As the five Kendall children grew up, thoughts of their mother were probably in their minds constantly. Having nowhere else to go, the children kept these thoughts to themselves. In 1961, however, the missing person case was reopened when one of the Kendall daughters went to the police after leaving home. Another sister came forward and made a statement as well. Together, they told the same shocking story of the night of August 2, 1952, when their mother disappeared.

Both girls declared that on that night, they had been sleeping in the bunk above their parents. They were awakened by the voice of their mother, screaming, "Don't Art! Oh, please don't!" They saw their father throw a bloody butcher knife onto the kitchen table, and drag his wife's body out of the cabin. The girls stayed where they were, shaking with fear. They did not dare move.

Their father was gone for about an hour and when he returned, he wiped up the blood with the bed sheets, gathered up the knife and his wife's clothing and then disappeared again. When he came back the second time, he scrubbed the cabin and told the children the *story* that they were to tell anyone who asked about the disappearance of their mother.

Arresting Kendall and charging him with the murder of his wife, although there was no body, created a sensational story. This had never been done before. The circumstantial evidence was so strong the lawyers knew they had just cause to try him and would probably win. The trial began October 22, 1961, and was soon completed. Arthur Kendall was found guilty of the murder and was sentenced to be hung.

Inside the county jail at Walkerton, the convicted prisoner was kept in solitary confinement, under constant visual guard in a cell that was lighted 24 hours a day. The local sheriff at the time was not happy about the coming execution. It was an era when groups had begun to pressure the Canadian judicial system to ban the death penalty. This time, though, it seemed there would be no reprieve. The sheriff had the duty of leading the hooded convict to the gallows and giving his assistance if needed.

An anonymous hangman, brought in specially for this hanging, was to be lodged at the Hartley House. Under his direction, two local carpenters chosen for the task were given the unusual contract to building a wooden scaffold and gallows in the

More Tales of the Unusual

exercise yard of the County of Bruce Jail. When they arrived at the jailyard to begin construction, they noticed that the heavy timbers were big enough and strong enough to hang an elephant. Taking up their hammers and saws, the two men began the arduous task ahead of them. Just as they began to follow the building plans, word was given to halt the proceedings.

Much to the relief of the sheriff, he would not have to contend with the newsworthy yet controversial hanging. There would be no hanging after all. The sentence had been changed to life imprisonment, the first sentence in Canada resulting from a "guilty" verdict without a body as evidence. It is noted that Kendall was released back to public life on parole, in 1975. There is no note telling whether his family have anything to do with him.

Some of the locals say there is the ghost of a female seen from time to time wandering the Bruce Peninsula around the Johnston Harbour area. She is supposedly buried under what is now a main highway. Maybe it's Helen Kendall looking to be reunited with her children.

Witching

Since pioneer times in Grey and Bruce, water witching, dowsing, or divining has been used to find water. By some people, it was once thought of as witchcraft, a gift of the devil.

The skill of water witching sometimes passed down through a family. Certain people seemed to have a sense of kinetic energy about them. The electrical energy in their bodies appears to have a joint effect with the energy from moving water, even if the water is underground. Dowsing was very rarely done for money. It was a "gift" to use, not to sell.

In ancient times, every village had a dowser. Others looked to them to find water in times of drought or when building homes. There was a man who farmed at Lake Charles who had this ability, as did a family who lived in Oxenden in the early 1900s. Their skills were highly regarded and much sought after as every family needed water, both for themselves and their livestock and crops. Water is the life source of the earth.

There are still some diviners in the area whose services continue to be used. A family in the Hepworth/Shallow Lake area made use of dowsers off and on for years. One man at Purple Valley has used his gift many times to find water acceptable for drilling. Others with the dowsing talent have passed away over the years. The ability to dowse

More Tales of the Unusual

for water is almost a lost art.

In our pioneer past, dowsing was done with a Y-shaped branch from a tree. Willow worked best because it is a water wood: that is, a tree that grows at the bank of a stream, pond, or place that is wetter than most. Some dowsers store their branch in water to keep it fresh for the next use. Ash or rowan was used as well. These branches were thought to have magical properties. Newlyweds planted trees in their garden or placed a twig or branch of the rowan (witchwood) over the top of each outside door of their home to bring good luck and to ward off evil spirits.

There is much more to dowsing than the ability to find water. Used almost since the beginning of time, it appears in wall drawings carbon-dated from around 1600 BC. No one knows for sure how dowsing works, just that it does. Many non-believers turn believers as they see for themselves how dowsing truly works. To succeed, you need to have the ability as well as the belief that you can make the rod work.

Keeping the rod at waist level, you hold closely but loosely onto the arms of the Y with the stem ending pointing level ahead of you. While holding the rod, ask out loud where the water is. The rod will do the work. You must be specific, asking for "a vein of potable water" for drinking or only for "running water" if it's for other purposes. Success is most likely when there is a need. The rod doesn't seem to work if the dowser is just showing off. When the rod finds water, a distinct downward pull will be felt. This is the direction of the water. The larger the amount of water, the stronger the pull.

More Tales of the Unusual

Hold on tight!

Reading material about dowsing past and present suggests a sort of magic about the ability to find water or minerals. Some dowsers also can find harmful emissions, noxious or radioactive, coming from under the ground. Their success has to do with the types and the mixture of minerals. Emissions can throw off the mineral or electrical flow in a human body. This means the body does not work at its peak performance, leaving cranky feelings, sleeping troubles, and sluggishness. Many people believe in the powers of the diviners, and use them before building a home.

It is said that almost anyone can dowse, or at least get a reaction from the rod they are holding. You might have to try various types of rods before you get the right one that is tuned to your body. Children in pre-teen years seem to have a better chance at a reading, because their minds are more open to new beliefs. Adults have minds less open to unusual or magical experiences. Try it. Who knows? you may have "the touch".

With Help from Ma Bell

The advertising that says, "A phone call is almost as good as being there" seems to be true in this story.

Following the death of her mother, Dee had her mother's wedding rings made into hoop earrings for her own newly pierced ears. She wore them fondly for several weeks until one day disaster struck.

About noon, Dee noticed that one earring was missing. Being busy on that day, she had already showered, been all over the house, worked in the carport, and gone down the lane. A lengthy search turned up the butterfly catch from the earring backing beside the bed. The earring itself seemed to have disappeared completely.

Several days went by while the distraught woman searched again and again. She felt as though her mother had reached from beyond the grave to take back the ring from her, as it had vanished completely. While discussing the problem, a friend suggested contacting a local psychic. Although she was not known for finding objects, perhaps she could help.

Dee phoned the psychic and asked her to come for an on-site visit of the home, to possibly assist in finding the ring through other means. As the psychic was unable to come to the house for several days, she offered to concentrate and have a "think" over

More Tales of the Unusual

the phone. After several minutes of silence, the psychic responded that she saw a cupboard, such as under a sink, where the earring had fallen from Dee's ear. This was a positive spot to look. She had also seen Dee holding a newborn or young child who gave her great joy. Finally, the psychic saw a symbol foretelling that the treasure would be found. Dee hung up, hopeful, and headed to the sink. The search proved fruitless. Sad to say, no earring was found.

Two days later friends came to visit. They brought with them a sister who hadn't been seen since the weekend of Dee's mother's death, and before that the weekend of Dee's father's death. After the visit, everyone was standing chatting in the laneway. The child of the couple poked around in the gravel beside their truck with his cap gun.

Suddenly the boy asked, "What's this?" They all stared at the shiny treasure in his hand. It was the lost earring. Dee rushed to hug the surprised child. All he had spied was the wire post when he started digging in the ground.

As everyone excitedly talked about the lost and found earring, Dee noticed the position of the site of the find. The boy was standing straight across the carport from a sink cupboard unit sitting outside. The "suggestion" that the psychic had given over the phone had actually come true.

The next day the psychic was able to come to Dee's . By the time Dee got down the stairs to greet her, the visitor was standing on the spot where the earring had been found. Staring at the cupboard in the back of the carport, she stated that it was the one she had "seen" through the phone lines. She

More Tales of the Unusual

was not at all surprised that the earring had been found. The young child she saw turned out to be the finder of the earring.

As Dee was telling me this story, I could tell she was vividly recalling the details from her interesting experience. It's amazing what types of information come over the telephone lines.

Suggested Reading

Driving Through Bruce County, Bruce County Historical Society, 1981.

Ghostly Lights - Great Lakes Tales of Terror, Annick Hivert-Carthew, illustrated by M. Diebboll & E. Bardsley, Wilderness Adventure Books, 1999.

Grey County's 125th Year 1825-1977, Compiled & edited by A.M. Rutherford, County Clerk; Updated by M. Bravener, Clerk-Treasurer, Administrator.

Haunted Ontario 2, Terry Boyle, Polar Bear Press, 1999.

Haunted Ontario, Terry Boyle, Polar Bear Press, 1998.

Historical Plaques and Cairns in Bruce County, Bruce County Historical Society, 1995.

Memories, Hazel L. Taylor, 1986.

Ontario Ghost Stories, Barbara Smith, Lone Pine Publishing, 1998.

Owen Sound Centennial 1857 - 1957 Souvenir Booklet.

Preserving the Peace - A History of the Owen Sound Police Force 1840-1990, Owen Sound Police Commission, 1990.

The Lovely Townships of Grey & Bruce - A series of talks written by A. Armitage and read on Radio Station CFOS-CFPS, Owen Sound, six booklets, 1972-1977.

More Tales of the Unusual

The Saddest Calamity - The wreck of the steamer J.H. Jones, Patrick Folkes, Bruce County Historical Society, 2000.

Yearbook, Shirley McClure, editor, Bruce County Historical Society, 2000.

You'll find many other books of local history and tales at bookstores and libraries throughout Bruce and Grey counties.

About the Author

Wiarton Photo Centre

Diane Madden has always loved to read. As a writer, she puts her thoughts on paper to express herself and to record stories for others to enjoy.

Diane lives with her family in the community of Clavering on Ontario's Bruce Peninsula. She has explored the hidden corners of Bruce and Grey counties, intrigued to poke in old cemeteries, visit museums and archives, and talk to residents old and young in her search for tales of the unexplained.

Diane's first book, *Tales of the Unusual: 'true' mysteries of Bruce and Grey,* was published by The Brucedale Press in 1998. She continues to collect tales and memories, and is working on stories for young children.

Do you know more tales?

Do you remember your grandparents? What stories did they tell? Perhaps it was about an abandoned house down the road, or memories of box socials in the schoolhouse, or revival meetings in a tent by the river. This is the history that no one wrote down, because these were such common happenings in the past.

I'd like to know how our grandparents' generation celebrated Hallowe'en. I'm looking for the ghost stories that were told for entertainment and explanation. What were people afraid of? Were there haunted houses?

What were the customs when someone died? Did family and neighbours gather at a wake or hang wreaths or crepe on the doors?

I'm also interested in the superstitions of past years. I have collected some, but many are different, depending on the ethnic background of the family.

I'd like to know about the skeletons in family closets. Who were they? Why were they considered the "black sheep" of the family?

If you have experiences or tales to share, please write to:

    Diane Madden
    R. R. # 3
    Hepworth, Ontario
    Canada N0H 1P0

More Tales of the Unusual

Don't miss Diane Madden's first collection, *Tales of the Unusual: 'true' mysteries of Bruce and Grey.*

From a haunted radio station in Owen Sound, to the classic legend of Spirit Rock, these 25 "tales with a tingle" will leave you wondering, *Could it be true?*

Roam again with Diane Madden on the highways and byways of Bruce and Grey Counties, looking for unsolved crimes, ghostly visitors, and mysterious strangers. You'll meet a man who waited fifty years for the solution to an airborne puzzle, and that weather prognosticator extraordinaire, the famed groundhog Wiarton Willie.

What the reviewers said about *Tales of the Unusual: 'true' mysteries of Bruce and Grey~*

...Madden has done a good job of writing about the myths and legends of this special place.~ Veronica Ross, *The Record,* Kitchener-Waterloo, Ontario.

...*a highly readable page-turner that will appeal to visitors and long-time residents alike. As she has written them, her stories are brooding and full of atmosphere but short on gore.* ~ Shawn Giilck, *Grey-Bruce This Week*

Look for it at your bookstore or library.

ISBN 1-896922-06-6   90 pages   quality softcover binding